WORLD'S UGLIEST DOG

Jeff Gottesfeld

SADDLEBACK
EDUCATIONAL PUBLISHING

red rhino
b OO k s®

With more titles on the way …

SADDLEBACK
EDUCATIONAL PUBLISHING
www.sdlback.com

ISBN-13: 978-1-62250-954-6
ISBN-10: 1-62250-954-4
eBook: 978-1-63078-177-4

Printed in Guangzhou, China
NOR/0515/CA21500875

19 18 17 16 15   1 2 3 4 5

Tana

Age: 12

Hobby: computer programming

Favorite School Subject: math

Greatest Fear: not qualifying for the national spelling bee

Best Quality: honesty

CHARACTERS

Storm

Age: unknown
Favorite Activity: taking a nap
Biggest Secret: can open the refrigerator
Favorite Food: ice-cold baby carrots
Best Quality: fun-loving

1
WOOF! WOOF!

Tana Glass had a spotted dog named Storm. She adopted him from the shelter. Storm's old name was Funky. Tana asked if a dog could learn a new name. The woman at the shelter said yes.

Storm got his new name that same day. It was snowing. The snow was two feet deep. Storm rolled in the snow. Tana laughed with joy.

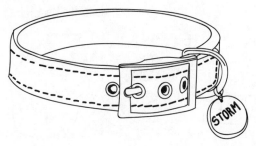

No other name seemed right. Storm seemed perfect. The dog learned it right away. Tana called to him in the snow.

"Here, Storm!"

Storm ran to her.

Tana was glad she had a dog. She had wanted one since she was little. Her parents had said no. Their house was too small.

It got better when Tana's big sister went to college. They had more room.

But first Tana's parents wanted to be sure that Tana would care for a dog. They made her get other pets to see how she did. A fish. A hamster. Tana did great. That's when her parents took Tana to the shelter.

Herb the hamster

Betty the betta

My other pets →

2

Storm turned out to be a great dog. He was smart and nice. He loved kids. He barked at odd sounds.

Tana was a shy sixth grader. She had few friends. Storm turned into her best friend. He was the best bud a girl could want.

There was only one bad thing about the dog. Storm was funny looking. In fact, he was super ugly. He had a big body and little legs. His tail was like a stick. His ears flopped. He had buckteeth. Worst of all, he drooled when he was happy.

He must be happy.

Everyone knew the ugly dog. People

came to see him when Tana took him out.
Some were not so nice.

"Dang, girl! That's an ugly dog!"

"Miss? Can I tell you something? Get that dog a mask!"

Something bad happened on one walk. They were near the park. Storm saw kids playing. He pulled because he wanted to say hi. Tana dropped his leash. Storm got free. He ran to the kids.

"Storm! Come back!" Tana called.

He didn't. Storm was too excited.

Tana called out, "It's fine! Don't worry! He's super nice!"

The kids looked up. They saw Storm.

"Look at that ugly dog! He has cooties! Run!" one kid screamed.

Storm looks even UGLIER when he runs.

The kids ran. Storm chased them. He was so happy.

Tana followed. "He does not have cooties! He just looks funny."

"Cooties! Cooties!" the kids all shouted.

Moms came running. They yelled at Tana. Tana got Storm and held him. Then she took him home.

Storm was still a good dog. But Tana wished that he was not so ugly.

2
THE LETTER

"Hi, honey. How was your walk?"

Tana's mom looked up. She was at her workbench. She made candles and sold them at fairs. Tana's dad was a police officer. The star of the family was Tana's big sister. She wanted to be a doctor.

Not just a doctor... a <u>BRAIN</u> surgeon!

"Um ... it was okay." Tana didn't want to

talk about what happened at the park. It was hard to admit that Storm scared kids.

Storm ran over to her mother. Her mom petted the dog between the ears. He loved that. He showed off his belly. Her mom petted him there too.

"Good." Her mom spread her arms wide. "I love the fall. Don't you? It's the best time to be outside."

Tana nodded. "Yeah. It's pretty cool."

The best thing about fall?

Pumpkin Spice Lattes (decaf)

← My favorite!

"You have homework?"

"Reading. Math. And I have to draw a map of the moon."

Her mom smiled. "That's good. Your own kids might live there one day." She snapped her fingers. "Oh! You got something in the mail today."

"Snail mail?"

I only get mail on my birthday.

TANA

Her mom nodded. "I'll get it. It's on the hall table."

While her mom went to the front hall,

9

Tana petted Storm. "You're a great dog. Don't let those kids get you down."

Storm licked her hand and drooled. Tana grinned and wiped away the slobber. Her dog wasn't thinking about the park at all. That was the great thing about dogs. They could focus on love.

Storm only thinks about love ... and food.

"Here you go," said Tana's mom. She gave Tana a big envelope. "I need to get back to work."

It was from a vet. Tana got stuff like this

all the time. But this one was not like all the others. It was an ad. But there was also a letter to her.

Dear Tana,

I am a vet who fixes how pets look. I can make an ugly pet look great. It is like a nose job for a person. It costs very little. In fact, it would cost you nothing. Your dog needs so much help that I would do it for free. I would like to take pictures. Before. And after. I would use them in an ad. Talk to your parents. Then call me.

Dr. John

There was a colored paper about Dr. John. He worked in town. And there was one more sheet of paper. It had note on it.

> *This may be good for Storm. He is a loser when it comes to looks. But it may help him win.*

It was an ad for a contest. The contest was called World's Ugliest Dog. Tana scanned the sheet. It would happen next weekend. At a hotel downtown.

The idea was to pick the ugliest dog in the world. The winner got a lifetime supply of dog food.

Set for life!

She looked at Storm. She was tired of people joking about her dog. She picked him up and held him like a baby. "Storm? You are not a loser. You are going to be a winner!"

3
BUBBA

Tana's parents said it was fine. They would pay the entry fee. Maybe Tana would make some new friends.

Tana found the entry forms on the Internet. The forms asked about Storm. What he liked to eat. How he liked to play. Even what breed he was. Tana wrote the truth. "My dog Storm is his own breed. The Storm breed." She even emailed a photo.

FUN FACT:
Storm once ate an
<u>ENTIRE</u> Thanksgiving
turkey!

The next day she got an email. Storm was good to go. He just needed papers from a vet. There was a list of approved vets. Dr. John was on the list.

"They don't want sick dogs," her mom said.

"That's fine. But let's not go to that Doctor John guy," Tana replied.

Tana and her mom took Storm to another vet. Tana went into the exam room with him. Her mom stayed in the lobby.

Storm needed shots. He was a brave dog. He did not make a sound when the needle went in. The vet gave him a treat after she was done.

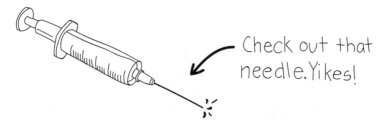

Check out that needle. Yikes!

"You've got a fine dog," the vet told Tana.

"So can he enter?" Tana asked.

"Yes, he can," the vet said. "You know, I've seen quite a few dogs for that contest. But yours is the ugliest by far. I think he's a winner."

First place, here we come!

"Thank you," Tana told her. "Know what's good?"

"What?"

"Storm doesn't care that he's ugly."

The vet chuckled. Tana went out to meet her mom in the waiting room.

"How did it go?" her mom asked.

Tana grinned. "Fine. Doctor Smith says Storm is so ugly he could win."

Storm's file:

Storm

UGLY

The vet's professional opinion

Just then, the front door to the vet's office opened. A girl and her dog came inside.

Tana and her mom checked out the new dog. Then they shared a look.

"Well, maybe Storm won't win after all," Tana joked.

The new dog was the size of a poodle. His coat was ginger. He had ears that stood up like a cat's. He had a giant belly and crooked teeth. He barked. It was more like a yelp than a bark.

"Nice dog," Tana told the girl.

The girl looked at her. They were about the same age. She had red hair like her dog. "Your dog looks nice too."

They match!

"Thanks."

"I'm Britt," said the girl. "This is Bubba. Don't ask how I got the name. I just like it. I'm entering him in a contest—"

"You mean for the the world's ugliest

dog?" Tana asked. "Me too! With my dog. I'm Tana. And this is Storm."

"Boy dog?"

Tana nodded. "Yep."

"Mine too," Britt said. "We don't have to worry about puppies."

Tana laughed. That was funny. She let Storm check out Bubba. The two dogs sniffed for a second. Then they started to play. They bumped, jumped, and barked.

"I guess our dogs like each other," Britt said.

"Maybe we can hang out before the contest," Tana told her.

"I'd like that."

Just like that, Tana made a new friend.

4
THE TRICK

"Go, dogs! Go!"

Britt threw the ball. Bubba and Storm chased it. They banged into each other as they tried to pick it up. Once. Twice. Three times.

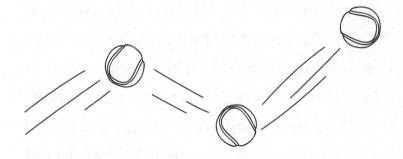

Then Storm grabbed the ball. He ran back to Britt and Tana. Storm dropped the ball at Tana's feet. He was happy with the game. Tana could tell from the drool. She wiped it off the ball.

GROSS!

"Your turn to throw," Britt told Tana.

Tana and Britt were now good friends. They had hung out all week. They went on walks. They went to the dog park. They lived close to each other. Just six blocks apart, in fact. But they did not go to the same school.

They were so different. Tana was tall and shy. Britt was small and bold. She would talk to anyone. Tana wished she could be like that.

"We need tricks for our dogs," Tana reminded her. "They have to do tricks for the contest. I don't think ball chasing will do. All dogs chase balls."

"Bubba can do all kinds of tricks," Britt told her. "Come here, Bubba."

Bubba ran to Britt. As Tana and Storm watched, Britt gave orders. Bubba rolled over one way. Then he rolled the other way. He did a front roll. He even did a back roll. A small crowd came to watch. They clapped when Britt and Bubba were done.

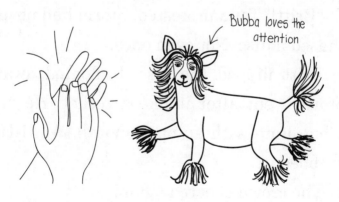

Bubba loves the attention

"That's an ugly dog," a guy told Britt. "But he's a smart one. What about the other dog?"

Britt smiled. "I don't know." She turned to Tana. "How about it? What can Storm do?"

Tana felt bad. Storm was a nice dog. But his big trick was shaking hands. That was not much of a trick at all.

Britt grabbed a Frisbee disc.

"He's a great disc dog," she told the man. "Watch."

"Britt!" Tana protested. Storm had never chased a disc. Not even once.

Britt flipped the disc. It floated away. Storm went after it like a rocket. He did a big jump with an open mouth. Wow! He grabbed it!

The crowd cheered again.

 24

Storm knew he had done well. He drooled on the Frisbee. Then he dropped it at Tana's feet. She threw it. She was good at Frisbee. It went far this time. Storm chased it. Perfect catch. There were more cheers.

Hm. That was easy. Storm had his trick for the contest.

Storm's hidden talent $\rightarrow$

5
TV STAR

The hotel lobby was full of ugly dogs. Tana had never seen so many. Big dogs. Small dogs. Black dogs. Brown dogs. Dogs so ugly they made Storm and Bubba look good. One of them was extra long, but with a round head. Tana heard his name was Hot Dog. He was the strangest dog Tana had ever seen.

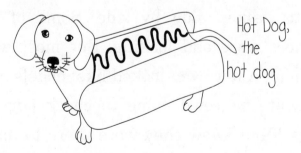

Hot Dog, the hot dog

It was the weekend before the contest. The organizers were throwing a party. They invited all the owners and their dogs. They asked radio and TV people to come too. They wanted people excited for the show.

Tana and Britt were there with Storm and Bubba. There were at least a hundred dogs and owners. They served burgers and hot dogs. The dogs got special chow.

These → Not These →

After the food was a parade. Tana and Britt walked side by side. Some of the owners were odd looking. But most were normal. A few even looked like models.

Quite a crowd came to check out the dogs. Tana knew they were there to make fun. Some made nasty jokes. But some came to pet Storm and Bubba. Bubba liked to be petted as much as Storm did.

One of the TV people came over to Tana and Britt. She was blonde. Tana knew her from the six o'clock news. She was followed by a big guy. He had the camera.

"Hi," said the woman. "I'm Karla Karlin. I'm from 4 News. Can I talk to you guys?" She turned to the camera guy. "Get some shots of the dogs, Bill. They're the real stars."

Tana had never been on TV. She wondered if her mom and dad would say it was okay. They weren't at the hotel. They had dropped off Tana and Storm. Then they went to dinner. She decided to text them.

"Let me ask my mom," Tana said. She saw Britt texting too.

Her mom texted right back. "Sure! Have fun!"

TONIGHT AT 6...

CHANNEL 4 Ugly Dogs and the Owners Who Love Them

Britt's mom said it was okay too. They sat down with Karla. The reporter asked all kinds of things. Did their dogs get made fun of? What care did an ugly dog need?

"Sure they get made fun of," Britt said.

"Everyone gets made fun of," Tana said.

"That's true," Karla agreed. "Even me."

"Anyway, ugly dogs are just dogs. They don't need extra care," Tana told her. "They may not have looks. But they have a lot of love."

They don't even look in a mirror.

"You'd get another ugly dog?" Karla asked Britt.

"Of course," Britt said. "I adopted Bubba, right?"

31

Tana spoke up. "It's not the dog's fault that it's ugly. It's just luck. Like with people. What matters isn't how a dog looks. What matters is how a dog acts."

The reporter grinned. "Can you show us how your dogs act?"

Tana turned to Storm. "Here, Storm!"

Britt called Bubba at the same time. "Here, Bubba!"

The dogs rested a few feet away. At the sound of their names, they bounded over. Then they covered Tana and Britt in dog kisses. Karla beamed.

Covered in kisses!

"Well then," Karla told the camera. "If you want love? Get an ugly dog. You may see me at the shelter on Monday. This is Karla Karlin, 4 News."

6
TOP TEN

It had been a great week. A lot of kids had seen the news. It made Tana a little famous. Kids came up to her to talk. They asked for dog advice. They asked to meet Storm. Some said they wanted to adopt ugly dogs too.

Tana was glad. She wondered if Dr. John had seen the news. She hoped he felt bad. How dare he fix dogs' faces! Tana wanted to write him a letter. She didn't. She gave Storm extra love instead. She also got him ready for the contest.

Getting Storm
Show-ready

DOG
GONE
CLEAN

Every day after school, they went to the dog park. They met Britt and Bubba there. Tana worked on Storm's Frisbee catching. The days were warm and clear. That helped.

Britt had taught Bubba a new trick. Now he could dance. He would get on his back legs. Then he would clap his front paws. Britt had him do it to the song "Black Dog." It was very cool.

Britt even taught Bubba to use tiny cymbals!

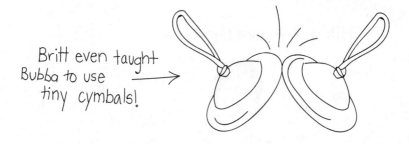

There were two parts to the World's Ugliest Dog. Saturday would be tricks. That part would be at the dog park. People could watch for free.

The next evening would be at the hotel. It was the big show. Each owner would walk his or her dog for the judges. It would just be the owner and the dog. The judges would choose twelve finalists. Then the finalists would compete for the crown.

There were three judges. One was an actor who had been born in town. Another was a baseball player. The third was a local vet.

His name was Dr. John.

What is HE doing here?

Tana could not believe it. Right before the tricks event, she told Britt about the letter Dr. John had sent.

Britt nodded. "I got one from him too. He thinks he's God's gift to ugly dogs."

"I don't like that guy!" Tana said.

"Well, tell him," said Britt.

Tana frowned. "He's a judge."

"Then tell him only if you have no chance to win. Come on. Let's get the dogs ready."

Many people had come to see the ugly dogs do tricks. Karla was there with her TV crew. Tana and Storm were the first up.

We go first? Talk about butterflies!

Dr. John spoke into a mic. Speakers made his voice boom. "Please welcome Tana and Storm to the tricks area!"

Tana was with her parents. She heard her name. She had three Frisbees in her right hand.

"Show your stuff!" her dad told her.

"You can do it!" her mom said.

They had their own cheering section!

Tana took Storm off the leash. She was scared in front of the crowd. What if Storm messed up?

He'll be the same dog, she told herself. *Relax.* "Okay, Storm," she told him. "Go!"

She flung one of the Frisbees. It floated

thirty yards. Storm ran it down. He jumped and got it in his mouth. Then he ran back to Tana and dropped it at her feet. The crowd cheered.

Tana had two more Frisbees. The trick was about to get even better.

"Okay, Storm," she told him again. "Go! Go!"

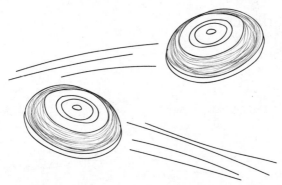

It had taken a lot of practice to get it right. Tana threw one Frisbee low to the right. Then she threw one high to the left. Storm chased after the first. He got it.

Then he spotted number two. He tracked

and grabbed it. He trotted back to Tana with both Frisbees in his jaws.

The crowd loved it. So did the judges. Dr. John even gave her a thumbs-up.

Karla came over. "We got that on tape," she told Tana.

Tana watched the rest of the tricks. Britt and Bubba did great. Bubba got the whole crowd dancing.

The crowd LOVED the skateboarding dog!

The judges talked when the tricks were over. A few minutes later, they ranked the dogs. Storm and Bubba were both in the top ten. The number one dog was the extra-long dog named Hot Dog. He had rolled over and over again.

Tana knew Storm could be in the finals. Never before had owning an ugly dog been so much fun.

7
REFUSED

Tana dressed nice for Sunday night. She put on a red dress and black shoes. Before they left for the hotel, she brushed Storm. He loved to be brushed. She brushed him for ten minutes. He looked great when she was done. He was the best ugly dog she had ever seen.

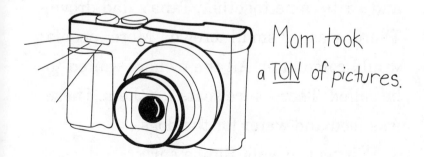

Mom took a <u>TON</u> of pictures.

"Are you going to win?" she asked.

He barked. Tana laughed. She wished she spoke "dog." It would be cool to know what he was saying.

I need one of these!

The Sunday event started at six. Tana and Britt came together. Tana's dad drove. There was a small crowd. More people would come later. All the owners waited to be called. There were seats for them. There was food and water for the dogs.

Britt got to walk Bubba early.

"Britt and Bubba to the circle! Britt and Bubba to the circle!"

"Good luck," Tana said.

Tana stood so she could see the action. Britt kept Bubba on the leash. He stayed right at her side. Britt ran a little bit. Bubba stayed with her.

Tana saw the judges. They liked Bubba. The small crowd did too. There was a lot of clapping. Bubba's huge ears perked up. He looked this way and that.

Will Bubba be the winner?

When they came back to the seats, Tana petted Bubba. "You guys did great."

47

Next up was Hot Dog. His owner was a very thin man. Britt said the dog and the man looked alike. They did great too. They even did an extra lap.

Tana waited for her name. And waited. Dog after dog got called. Storm did not like the wait. He moved around a lot. Then he licked his paws. He did that when he was bored.

This is taking too long!

"It's okay, Storm." Tana scratched him. That helped. A little.

Storm was the very last dog to be called to the ring.

"Tana and Storm! Please come to the circle. Tana and Storm to the circle."

"Come on, Storm," Tana said.

She got to her feet. Storm stood too. But he didn't move.

"Storm? Come on."

Tana gave him a little tug. He did not budge.

"Tana and Storm!" The call came again.

"Come on, boy," Tana urged.

Storm held firm.

"Okay. Let's go to Plan B." Tana picked up her dog. That's when Storm moaned. Loud. As if Tana was hurting him. Tana did not speak dog. But she got what he was saying. Storm did not want to do this.

And she did not know if she could make him.

8
THE DROPOUT

Tana did the right thing. She put him down. Storm pulled away.

She gave it one more try.

"Come on, Storm," she told him. "This is your chance to shine!"

He didn't budge. She had one more shot. There were two doggie cookies in her pocket. He loved those. She took out one to show him. She was sure he would come for it.

← Turkey flavor, his favorite!

Nothing.

"Storm?"

It was crazy. But it seemed like Storm shook his head to say no.

There were two contest staff members near her. One came over to help.

"Looks like you have a stubborn dog," she said.

"He's never like this," Tana moaned.

The woman smiled. "Dogs have minds of their own. Maybe there is something he wants to do more than go into the ring."

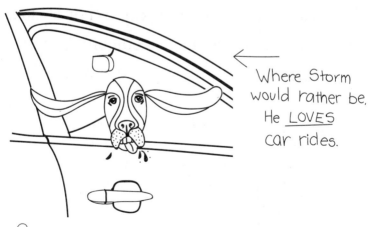

Where Storm would rather be. He LOVES car rides.

Tana felt her cheeks go red. This was the worst. Storm was ruining everything.

My face looked like a tomato!

Finally, one of the judges spoke into a mic. "Let's move on with the show. Thank you, Tana! Thank you, Storm! We'll announce the final five after a short break."

That was it. Tana knew her contest was over. She had to drop out. She felt ready to cry. Then Storm looked at her with big eyes.

"It's okay," she said to the dog. She held her arms open. The dog came to her.

"Is everything okay?"

Tana turned around. There was Britt and Bubba. Behind them were Tana's parents. They all looked worried.

They were holding gifts:

Flowers for me →

← A toy for Storm

"It's fine," Tana told them. "Storm just got cold feet. He didn't want to go out there. I tried everything."

"Yikes," Britt said. "He's okay, right?"

Tana looked at her dog. He met her gaze.

"Want that cookie now?" Tana asked.

The dog barked happily and came to her. He looked relaxed. There was no worry in his eyes. She offered him the cookie. He chomped it happily.

Tana nodded. She was out of the contest. But her dog was fine. And that was the only thing that really mattered.

9
SMOKE!

"Do you want to stay?" asked Tana's mom. "We can see how Britt does."

Tana thought for a moment. Part of her wanted to stay. But what about Storm? He was not a person. He didn't care. Her dog would just feel trapped. She had to think about his feelings too. She went to Britt.

← Dogs don't care about winning.

WINNER

"Will you mind much if I take Storm home? I don't think he wants to watch. If I were him, I'd rather go home."

I think he is ready for a nap.

"He's had a long night. My parents are coming soon to watch." Britt grinned. "I order you to take Storm for a long walk. Here's the thing. Storm doesn't care who wins. We are the only ones who care. All he wants is to be a good dog. Same thing with Bubba."

"Text me. Tell me how it goes. And I'll watch the news," Tana said.

"You got it," Britt said.

The two girls hugged. As Tana and her

parents left, Karla Karlin came up to them in the hall.

"Tana! Are you okay? We were all set for Storm. What happened?"

Tana shook her head. "I don't know. I think you'll have to ask Storm."

Karla kneeled by Storm. She got her mic and put it near his face. "So, Storm. Can you tell me why didn't you want to do the walk?"

Too many questions!

CHANNEL 4

Storm gave two happy barks. He licked Karla's face. Then he drooled. Everyone laughed, even Karla. The reporter turned to Tana. "I'm sorry you're not in the finals. You've got a great ugly dog. May he live a long ugly life."

"Thank you."

They all said goodbye.

After that, Tana and her parents walked down a long hall. It led to the parking lot. As they neared the doors, Storm stopped. He looked left and right. Something was bugging him.

"What's up, Storm?" Tana asked.

Storm tilted his head. He sniffed. Then he sniffed again.

"What's up? What do you smell, Storm?"

Storm pulled at his leash. Tana followed him. As she did, she smelled a scary odor.

Smoke! It came from under a door in the hall.

"There's a fire!" Tana yelled. "Call 911!"

She saw a fire alarm on the wall. She pulled it. Bells clanged. A moment later, the door opened. Smoke poured into the hall. A few people stepped out. They were coughing.

Her parents told Tana to leave the hotel. But Tana needed to know one thing.

"Is there anyone else in that room?" she asked.

Storm pulled at the leash. He wanted to go into the smoky room.

"No, Storm," said Tana. "Stay with me."

Storm gave a huge pull. Just like at the park, he yanked the leash from Tana's hand. Then he ran into the smoky room.

Tana screamed. "No! Stop him! He'll die!"

Stay away from there, Storm!

10
THE WINNER

"There's six more people in there!"

"We were having a meeting!"

"It started smoking near the door!"

"The room filled with smoke!"

Tana was now outside the hotel. So was everyone else. There were lots of people. Some had been in the smoky room. Firefighters had come. They were dressed in full gear.

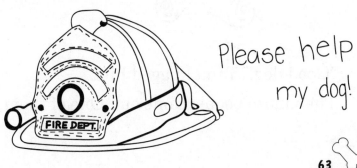

Please help my dog!

"There are people in there," Tana had told them. "And my dog!"

The firefighters went in. A few moments later, people started coming out. Tana counted them. One, two, three, four, five, and six.

Tana was scared for Storm. But then the firefighters led him outside. He smelled of smoke. His eyes were red. That was it. He dragged his leash.

Storm
smells like a
campfire

"Good dog!" Tana hugged him.

Then more people came out. One of them

came to Tana. "Your dog saved our lives. We followed his barks. He got us out!"

A firefighter joined them. "Fire in the wall. So much smoke. But it's over. All clear. Hey. This is your dog?"

"Yes, sir," Tana told him. "He's mine."

"When we got in? He was with the people in the room. He helped get them out. This dog is a hero."

HERO!

"How could he even see?" Tana asked.

The firefighter wiped his face. "I don't know." He touched Storm under his jaw.

"You helped us. Thanks, buddy. You did good. What a great dog."

"Um, Tana? Excuse me?"

Tana turned to her left. There stood Dr. John. He had come over to see what was going on.

"Yes?" asked Tana.

"I want to say sorry. I had no right to send you that letter. Your dog is fine just how he is."

I should make him apologize to Storm.

Tana eyed him. "Thank you. And?"

"And what?" Dr. John asked.

"And you will never send another letter.

To anyone. Because all dogs are fine just how they are. Just like people."

Dr. John frowned. "I didn't say that."

Tana stared hard. "That's too bad. Come on, Storm. Bye!"

It felt great to walk away from Dr. John.

Tana and her family did not go home. They went back to the ballroom. The judges wanted to give Storm a special prize. They gave it out just after the main awards. In those awards, Bubba had placed third. The big winner was Hot Dog. It was not even close. He did his big roll when he won.

Karla from 4 News gave the special prize. Tana waited with Storm just off the stage.

"There's one more ugly dog here tonight. He isn't cute. But he's strong. He's brave.

And he saves lives. He needs a prize of his own. Come on up! Tana and her dog, Storm!"

Tana had Storm on his leash. She took Storm to the stage. The crowd stood and cheered. Karla gave Tana a red ribbon. Tana draped it over Storm. The dog barked twice. The crowd loved it. Britt was still on the stage with Bubba. She came over to hug Tana. The two dogs licked each other's faces. The crowd loved it more.

Storm had not won World's Ugliest Dog. But he was still a big winner.